SWEET LAND OF LIBERTY

Ω

Published by
PEACHTREE PUBLISHERS
1700 Chattahoochee Avenue
Atlanta, Georgia 30318-2112
www.peachtree-online.com

Text © 2007 by Deborah Hopkinson
Illustrations © 2007 by Leonard Jenkins

Book design by Leonard Jenkins
Cover design and art direction by Loraine M. Joyner
Illustrations created in mixed media on chipboard; text typeset in
International Typeface Corporation's Stone Serif; titles and initial
capitals typeset in Letraset's Revue.

Printed and manufactured in Singapore
10 9 8 7 6 5 4 3 2 1
First Edition

Library of Congress Cataloging-in-Publication Data

Hopkinson, Deborah.
  Sweet land of liberty / written by Deborah Hopkinson ; illustrated
by Leonard Jenkins.
    p. cm.
  ISBN 978-1-56145-395-5
  1. United States—Race relations—History—20th century—
Anecdotes—Juvenile literature. 2. African Americans—Civil rights—
History—20th century—Anecdotes—Juvenile literature. 3.
Chapman, Oscar L. (Oscar Littleton), 1896-1978—Anecdotes—
Juvenile literature. 4. Anderson, Marian, 1897-1993—Anecdotes—
Juvenile literature. 5. Concerts—Washington (D.C.)—History—20th
century—Juvenile literature. 6. Lincoln Memorial (Washington,
D.C.)—Anecdotes—Juvenile literature. 7. African Americans—
Biography—Anecdotes—Juvenile literature. I. Jenkins, Leonard, ill.
II. Title.
  E185.61.H83 2007
  973'.0496073—dc22
                    2006024331

For Anne, Will, Lydia, and Charlotte,
who love to read—and sing.

—D. H.

SWEET LAND OF LIBERTY

WRITTEN BY
Deborah Hopkinson

ILLUSTRATED BY
Leonard Jenkins

Ω
PEACHTREE
ATLANTA

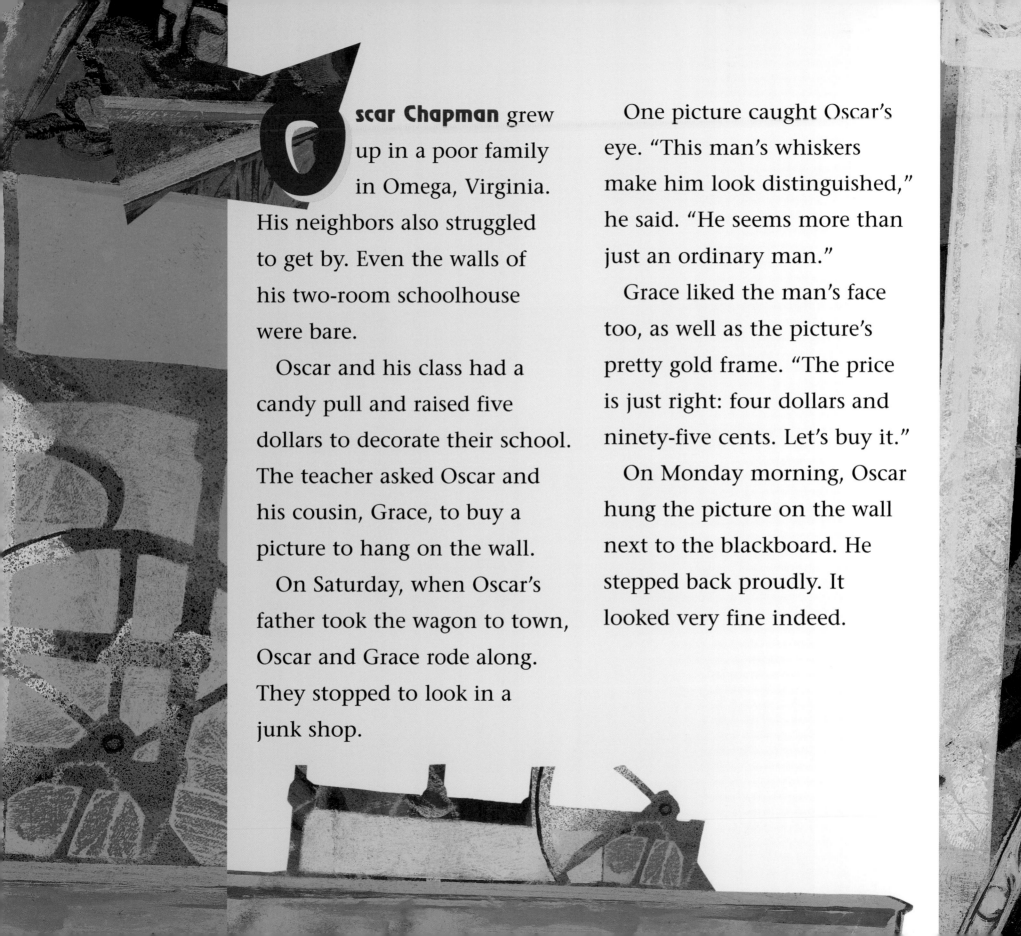

Oscar Chapman grew up in a poor family in Omega, Virginia. His neighbors also struggled to get by. Even the walls of his two-room schoolhouse were bare.

Oscar and his class had a candy pull and raised five dollars to decorate their school. The teacher asked Oscar and his cousin, Grace, to buy a picture to hang on the wall.

On Saturday, when Oscar's father took the wagon to town, Oscar and Grace rode along. They stopped to look in a junk shop.

One picture caught Oscar's eye. "This man's whiskers make him look distinguished," he said. "He seems more than just an ordinary man."

Grace liked the man's face too, as well as the picture's pretty gold frame. "The price is just right: four dollars and ninety-five cents. Let's buy it."

On Monday morning, Oscar hung the picture on the wall next to the blackboard. He stepped back proudly. It looked very fine indeed.

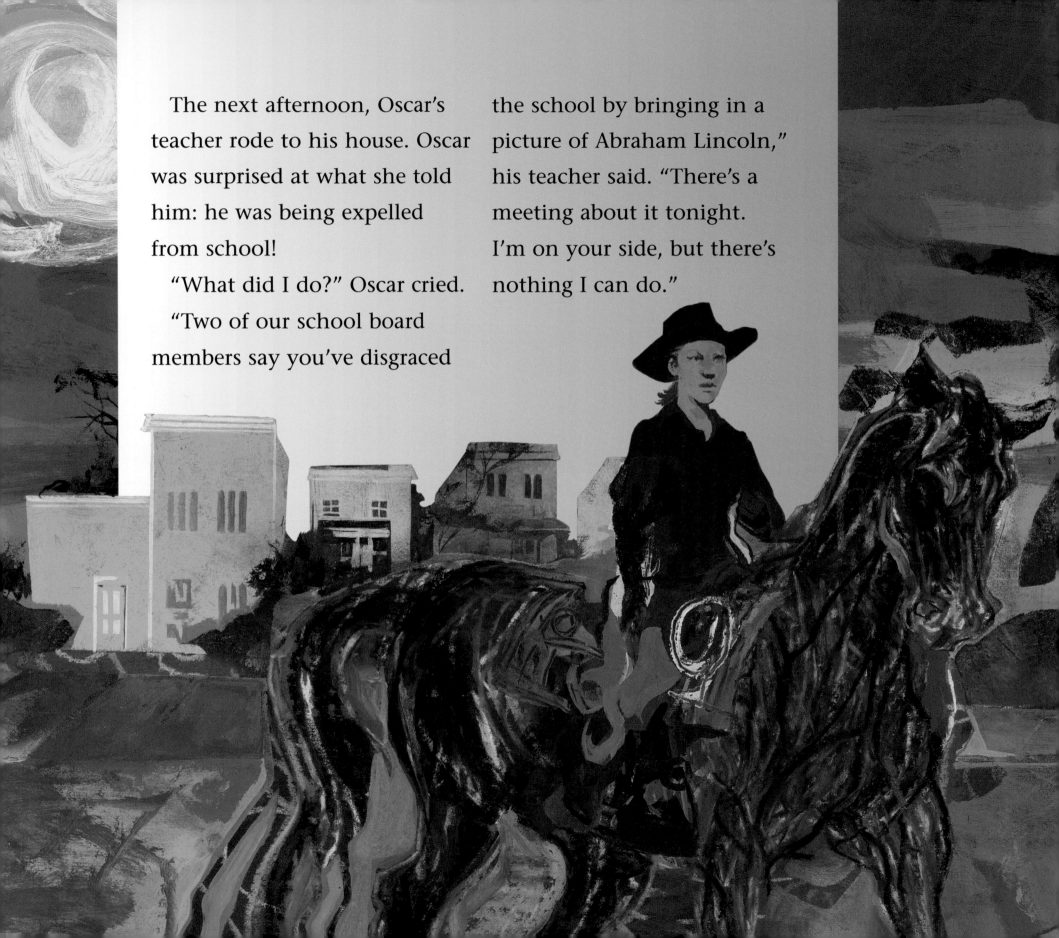

The next afternoon, Oscar's teacher rode to his house. Oscar was surprised at what she told him: he was being expelled from school!

"What did I do?" Oscar cried.

"Two of our school board members say you've disgraced the school by bringing in a picture of Abraham Lincoln," his teacher said. "There's a meeting about it tonight. I'm on your side, but there's nothing I can do."

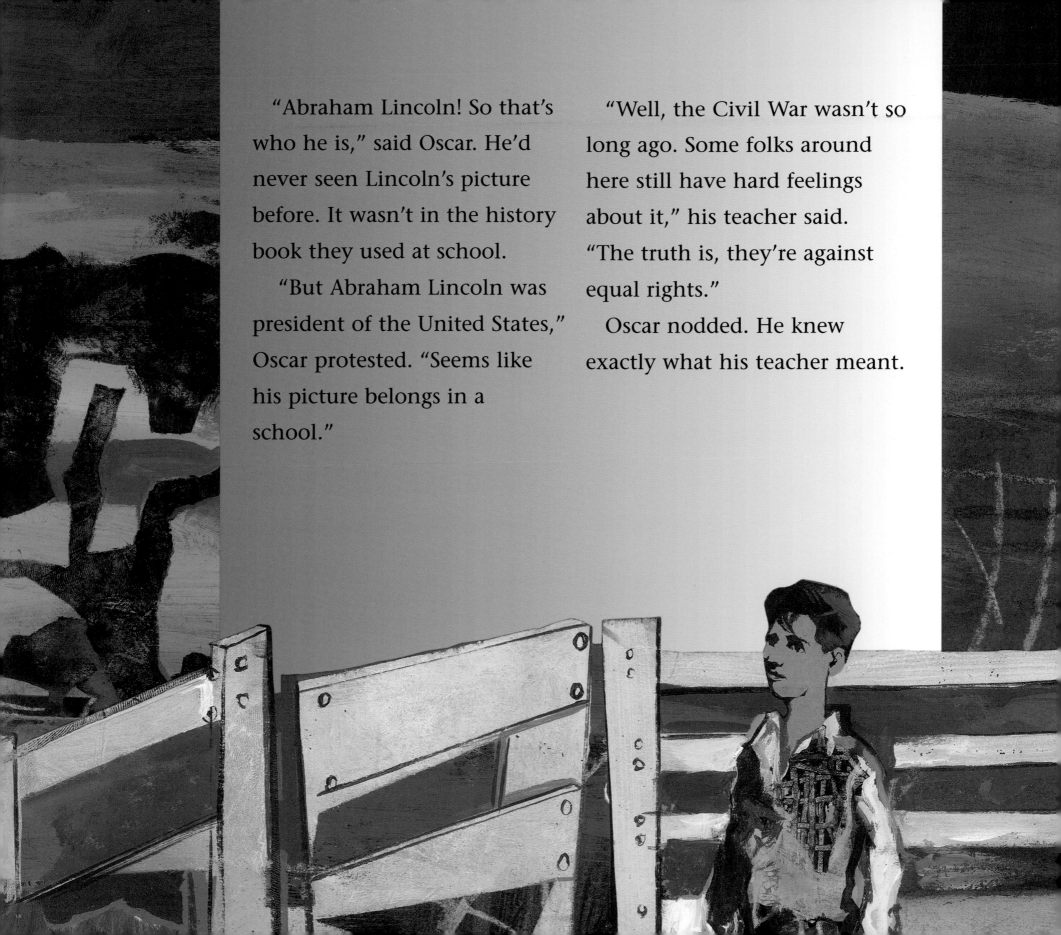

"Abraham Lincoln! So that's who he is," said Oscar. He'd never seen Lincoln's picture before. It wasn't in the history book they used at school.

"But Abraham Lincoln was president of the United States," Oscar protested. "Seems like his picture belongs in a school."

"Well, the Civil War wasn't so long ago. Some folks around here still have hard feelings about it," his teacher said. "The truth is, they're against equal rights."

Oscar nodded. He knew exactly what his teacher meant.

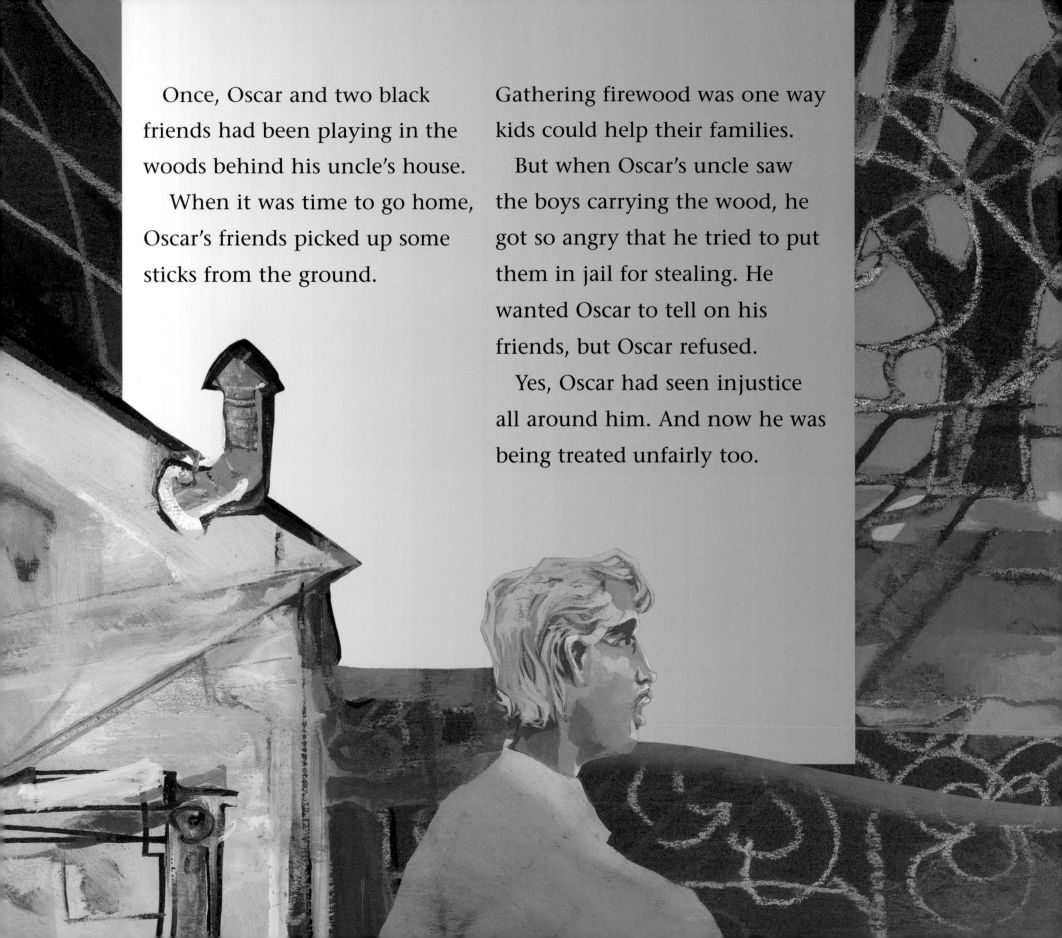

Once, Oscar and two black friends had been playing in the woods behind his uncle's house.

When it was time to go home, Oscar's friends picked up some sticks from the ground.

Gathering firewood was one way kids could help their families.

But when Oscar's uncle saw the boys carrying the wood, he got so angry that he tried to put them in jail for stealing. He wanted Oscar to tell on his friends, but Oscar refused.

Yes, Oscar had seen injustice all around him. And now he was being treated unfairly too.

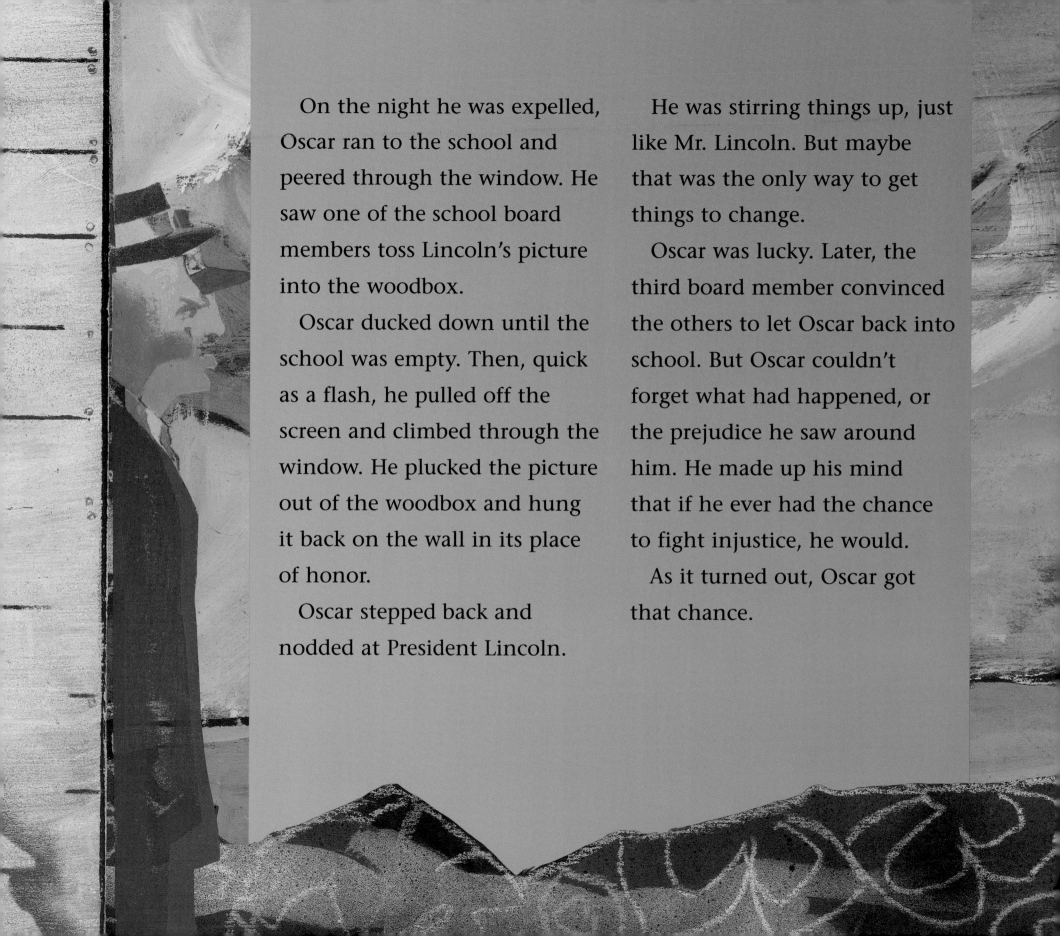

On the night he was expelled, Oscar ran to the school and peered through the window. He saw one of the school board members toss Lincoln's picture into the woodbox.

Oscar ducked down until the school was empty. Then, quick as a flash, he pulled off the screen and climbed through the window. He plucked the picture out of the woodbox and hung it back on the wall in its place of honor.

Oscar stepped back and nodded at President Lincoln.

He was stirring things up, just like Mr. Lincoln. But maybe that was the only way to get things to change.

Oscar was lucky. Later, the third board member convinced the others to let Oscar back into school. But Oscar couldn't forget what had happened, or the prejudice he saw around him. He made up his mind that if he ever had the chance to fight injustice, he would.

As it turned out, Oscar got that chance.

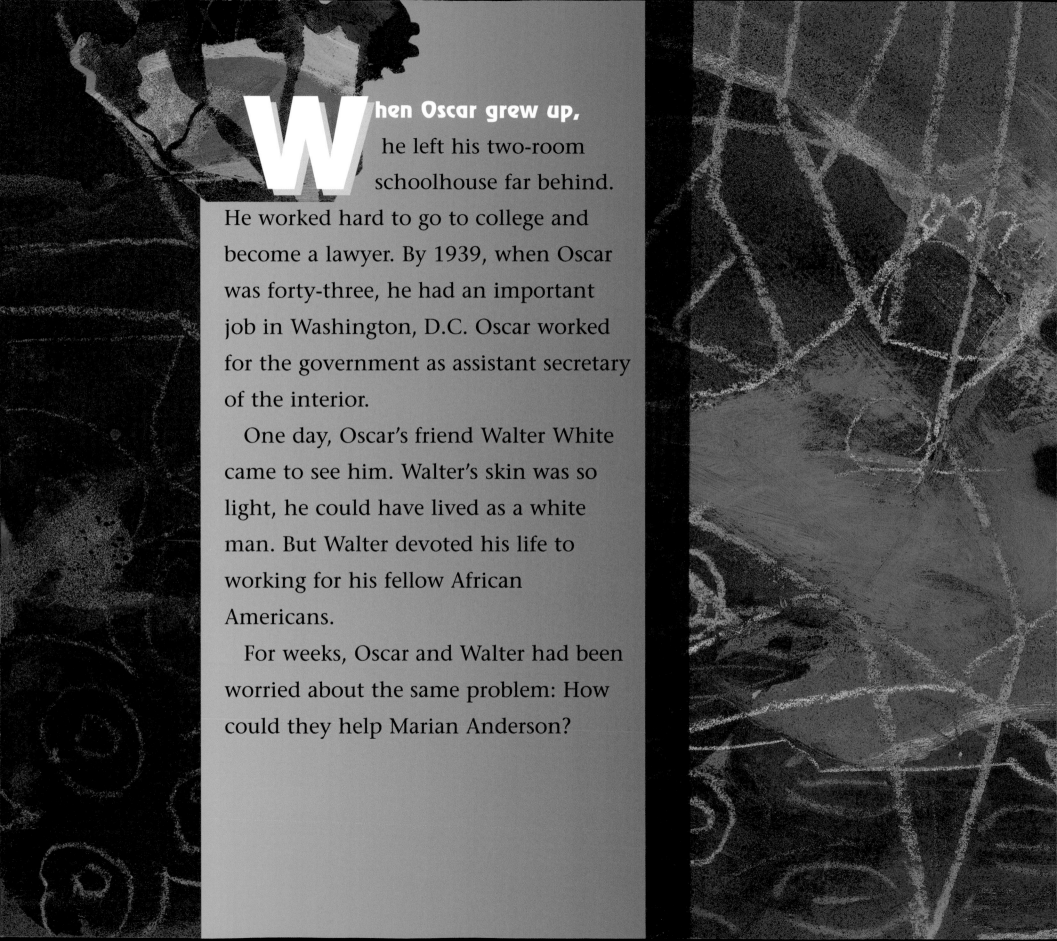

When Oscar grew up, he left his two-room schoolhouse far behind. He worked hard to go to college and become a lawyer. By 1939, when Oscar was forty-three, he had an important job in Washington, D.C. Oscar worked for the government as assistant secretary of the interior.

One day, Oscar's friend Walter White came to see him. Walter's skin was so light, he could have lived as a white man. But Walter devoted his life to working for his fellow African Americans.

For weeks, Oscar and Walter had been worried about the same problem: How could they help Marian Anderson?

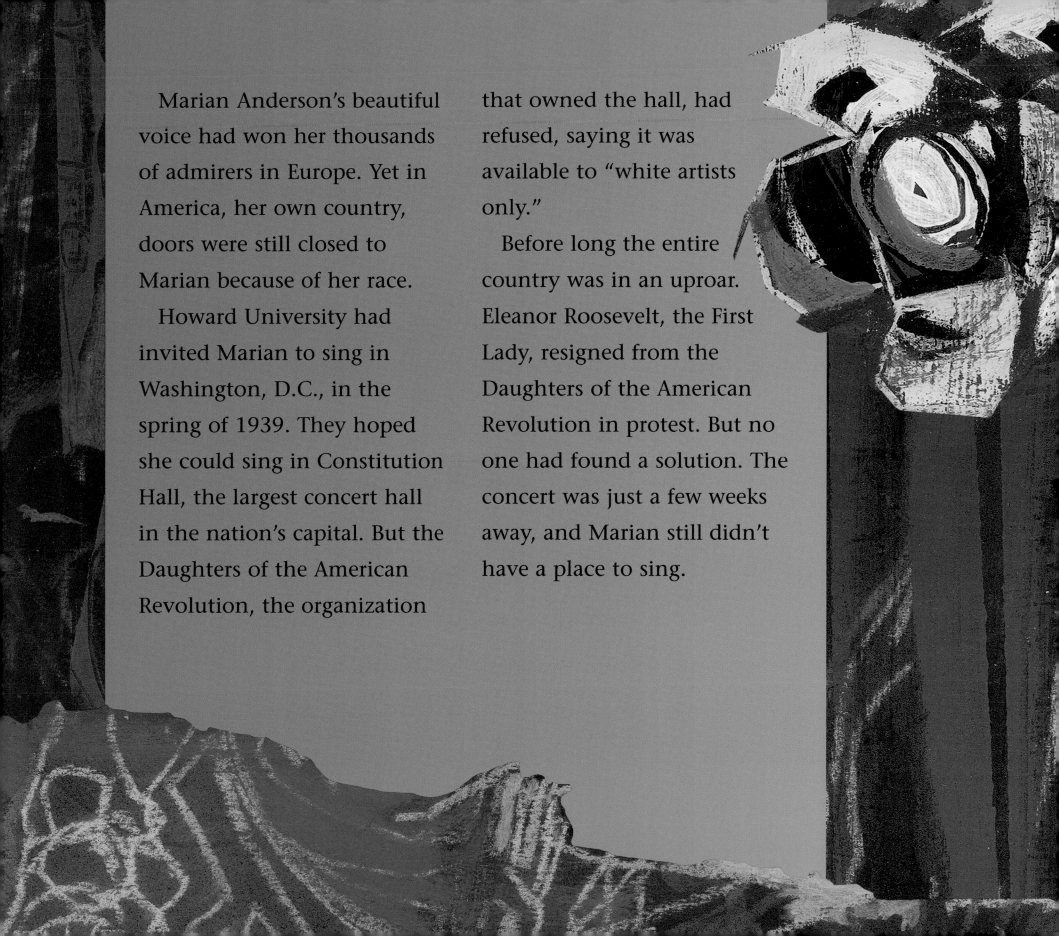

Marian Anderson's beautiful voice had won her thousands of admirers in Europe. Yet in America, her own country, doors were still closed to Marian because of her race.

Howard University had invited Marian to sing in Washington, D.C., in the spring of 1939. They hoped she could sing in Constitution Hall, the largest concert hall in the nation's capital. But the Daughters of the American Revolution, the organization that owned the hall, had refused, saying it was available to "white artists only."

Before long the entire country was in an uproar. Eleanor Roosevelt, the First Lady, resigned from the Daughters of the American Revolution in protest. But no one had found a solution. The concert was just a few weeks away, and Marian still didn't have a place to sing.

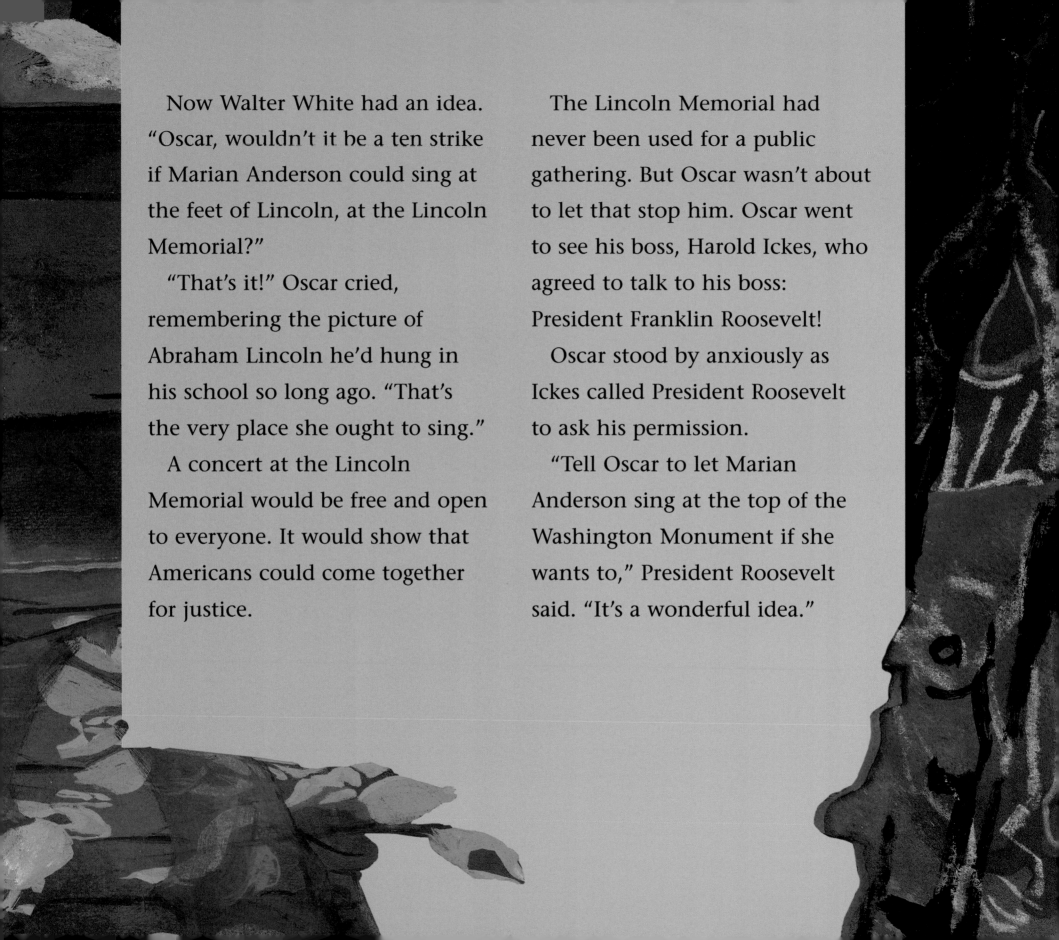

Now Walter White had an idea. "Oscar, wouldn't it be a ten strike if Marian Anderson could sing at the feet of Lincoln, at the Lincoln Memorial?"

"That's it!" Oscar cried, remembering the picture of Abraham Lincoln he'd hung in his school so long ago. "That's the very place she ought to sing."

A concert at the Lincoln Memorial would be free and open to everyone. It would show that Americans could come together for justice.

The Lincoln Memorial had never been used for a public gathering. But Oscar wasn't about to let that stop him. Oscar went to see his boss, Harold Ickes, who agreed to talk to his boss: President Franklin Roosevelt!

Oscar stood by anxiously as Ickes called President Roosevelt to ask his permission.

"Tell Oscar to let Marian Anderson sing at the top of the Washington Monument if she wants to," President Roosevelt said. "It's a wonderful idea."

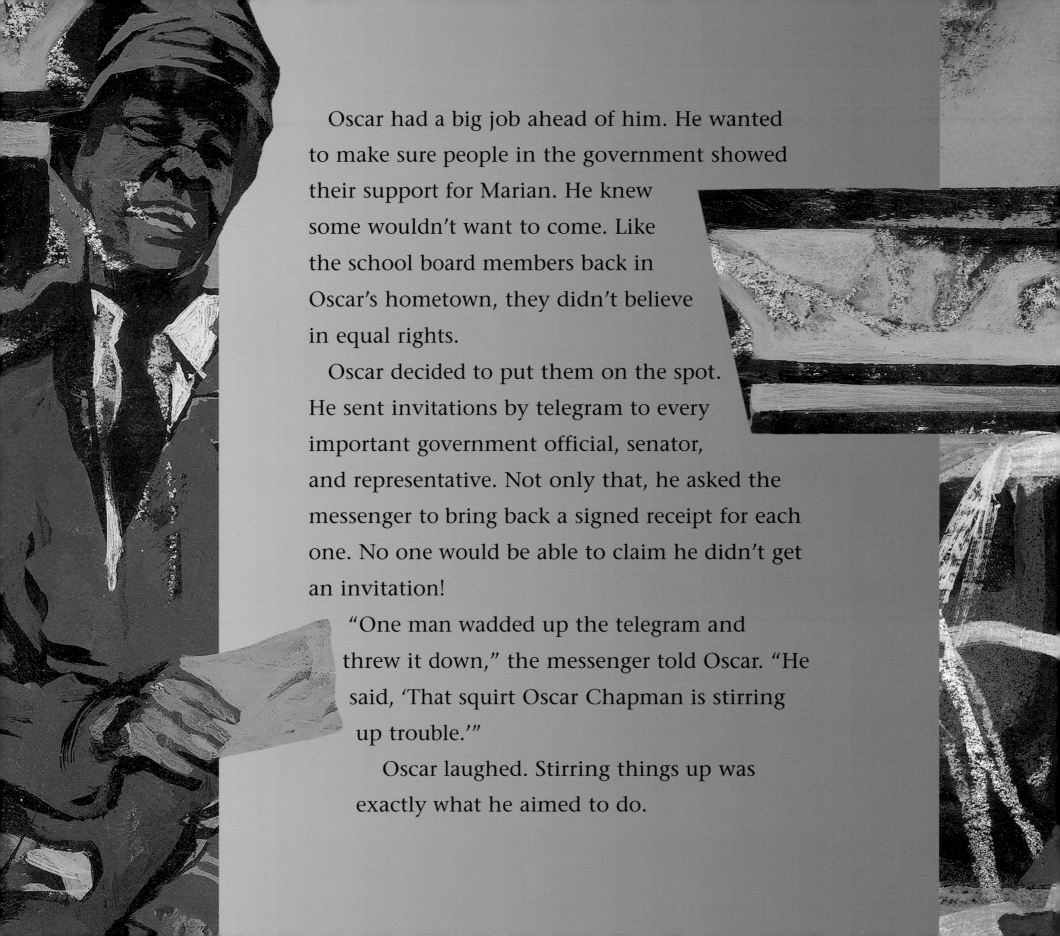

Oscar had a big job ahead of him. He wanted to make sure people in the government showed their support for Marian. He knew some wouldn't want to come. Like the school board members back in Oscar's hometown, they didn't believe in equal rights.

Oscar decided to put them on the spot. He sent invitations by telegram to every important government official, senator, and representative. Not only that, he asked the messenger to bring back a signed receipt for each one. No one would be able to claim he didn't get an invitation!

"One man wadded up the telegram and threw it down," the messenger told Oscar. "He said, 'That squirt Oscar Chapman is stirring up trouble.'"

Oscar laughed. Stirring things up was exactly what he aimed to do.

On Easter Sunday, April 9, 1939, people gathered early near the Lincoln Memorial. Thousands came in buses from Philadelphia, Marian Anderson's hometown.

At first the day was cold and cloudy. But soon the sky cleared. By five o'clock, when the concert was set to begin, the crowd stretched from the Lincoln Memorial to the Washington Monument.

Constitution Hall, where Marian Anderson had hoped to sing, could seat 4,000 people. But now 75,000 people of all ages and races would hear her.

When Marian stepped forward, she looked out on a vast sea of faces. She could feel a great wave of good will pouring out from everyone. She took a deep breath, and sang from her heart.

Marian chose to begin by singing not just about, but to the country she loved, changing the words of a beloved old song. A hush came over the crowd as her powerful voice rang forth.

My country, 'tis of thee,

Sweet land of liberty,

To thee we sing;

Land where my fathers died,

Land of the pilgrims' pride,

From every mountainside

Let freedom ring!

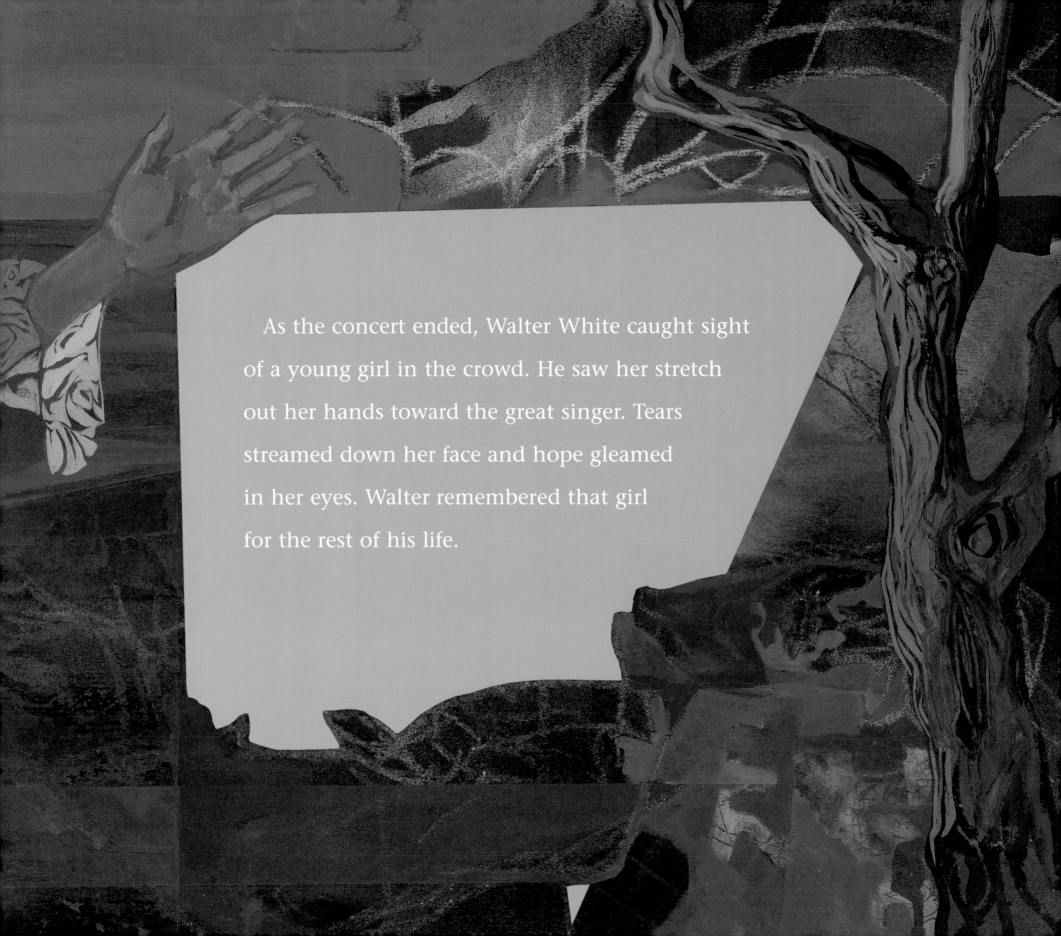

As the concert ended, Walter White caught sight of a young girl in the crowd. He saw her stretch out her hands toward the great singer. Tears streamed down her face and hope gleamed in her eyes. Walter remembered that girl for the rest of his life.

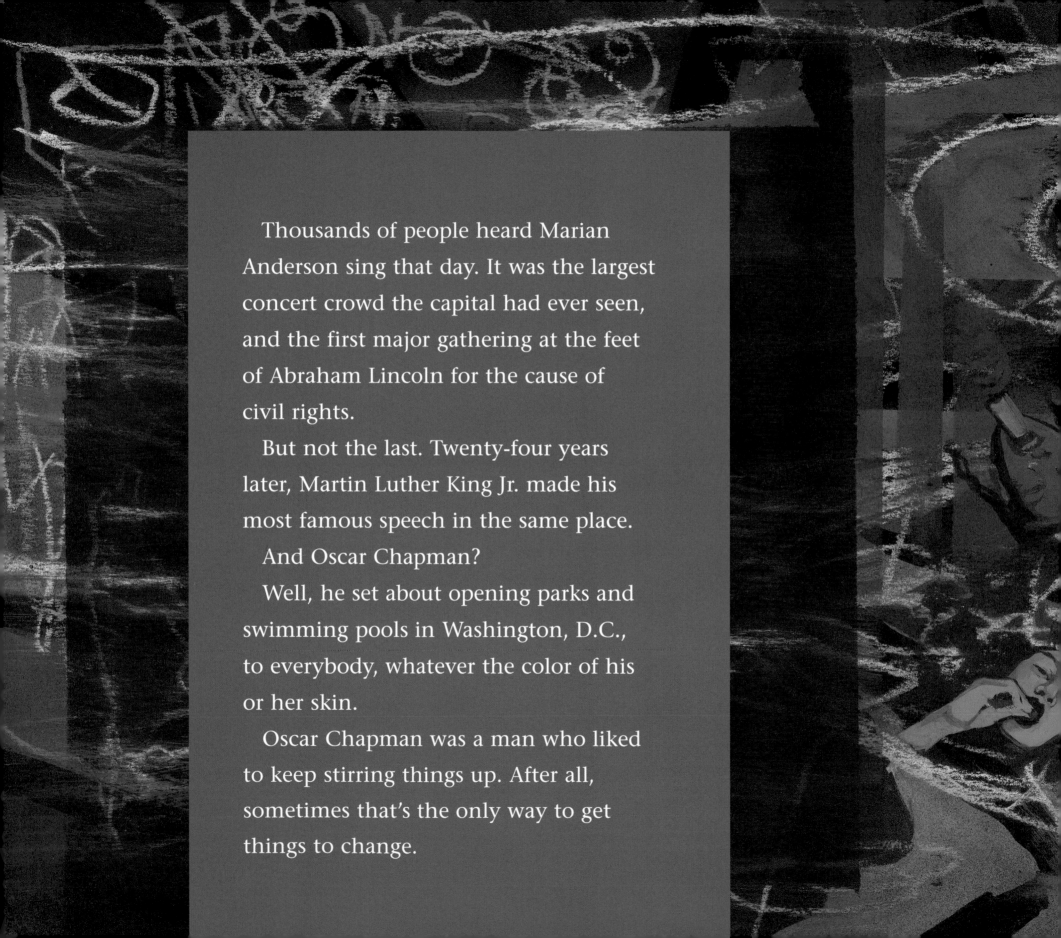

Thousands of people heard Marian Anderson sing that day. It was the largest concert crowd the capital had ever seen, and the first major gathering at the feet of Abraham Lincoln for the cause of civil rights.

But not the last. Twenty-four years later, Martin Luther King Jr. made his most famous speech in the same place.

And Oscar Chapman?

Well, he set about opening parks and swimming pools in Washington, D.C., to everybody, whatever the color of his or her skin.

Oscar Chapman was a man who liked to keep stirring things up. After all, sometimes that's the only way to get things to change.

MARIAN ANDERSON AT
THE LINCOLN MEMORIAL,
EASTER SUNDAY, 1939

Author's Note

Ever since I saw a photograph of Marian Anderson on the steps of the Lincoln Memorial, I've wondered what it would have been like to have been present at a moment when so many people came together to celebrate a great singer and make a stand for justice and equal rights.

To learn more, I wrote to the University of Pennsylvania, where Marian Anderson's papers are kept. As I read the newspaper clippings they sent, I came across a name I'd never heard: Oscar Chapman (1896–1978). It was Mr. Chapman, one article reported, who suggested the concert be held at the Lincoln Memorial because of something that happened to him as a child.

Who was Oscar Chapman? I wondered. I found an oral history interview with him in the Harry S. Truman Presidential

Museum and Library in Independence, Missouri. When I got those five bound volumes through interlibrary loan (they are now on the web at *www.trumanlibrary.org*), I couldn't wait to start reading. Mr. Chapman had a long and distinguished career in government. Would he mention something that had happened to him when he was twelve years old?

Sure enough, in an interview on August 2, 1972, Oscar Chapman recounted his experience of being expelled from school. Clearly, living in a community where prejudice and intolerance existed had a profound effect on Mr. Chapman's life.

I also read Marian Anderson's autobiography, MY LORD, WHAT A MORNING; her biography, MARIAN ANDERSON: A SINGER'S JOURNEY by Allan Keiler; and A MAN CALLED WHITE: THE AUTOBIOGRAPHY OF WALTER WHITE, in which the author writes of his childhood in Atlanta and his years working for civil rights.

In his book, Mr. Keiler notes that others along with Mr. Chapman were interested in having Marian sing at a public concert, including her longtime manager, Sol Hurok; officials from Howard University; and Walter White, head of the National Association for the Advancement of Colored People.

It appears that Walter White first suggested the idea of the Lincoln Memorial to Oscar Chapman. Oscar agreed, recalling

OSCAR CHAPMAN

WALTER WHITE

OSCAR CHAPMAN, MARIAN ANDERSON, AND MRS. HAROLD ICKES IN 1952

his own childhood experience with Abraham Lincoln's picture, and worked hard to make the concert a reality. Marian Anderson's powerful rendition of "America," often known by its first line, "My Country, 'Tis of Thee," is available at *www.library.upenn.edu/exhibits/rbm/anderson/lincoln.html.*

If you listen carefully, you can hear her change the lyrics, singing "To thee we sing," instead of the traditional "Of thee I sing." Marian Anderson knew well that America had much work ahead to "let freedom ring."

Learning about Oscar Chapman helped me to realize how much things that happen to us as children can change our lives.

Sometimes we go on to change other lives. And every once in a while, we might even change the course of history.

MARIAN
ANDERSON
PERFORMS AT
THE LINCOLN
MEMORIAL